THE PATH OF

JESUS

📖 Bible story for kids 📖

Story for
children about
the life of jesus

1

Dear reader,

We would like to give you our most sincere thanks for purchasing our book. We hope it will provide you with hours of learning and entertainment.

If you find that you love our book and feel inclined to share your thoughts with others, we would greatly appreciate it if you could take a few minutes to write a review. Your feedback and support is essential to us as independent publishers, and it would be very important for us to hear your thoughts.

Once again, thank you for your support and for choosing our book. We hope you continue to enjoy our content, and we look forward to hearing from you soon.

Best regards, DoubleD Editorial Team.

TABLE OF CONTENT

TABLE OF CONTENT.2

TABLE OF CONTENT

TABLE OF CONTENT.2

INTRODUCCION

Hello! Did you know that reading a story about the life of Jesus can be very exciting and at the same time a great learning opportunity? Through reading, you can learn more about Christian history and values, such as peace, love, and forgiveness. Plus, you'll discover how Jesus lived his life, how he helped others, and how he shared messages of peace and love. You will also acquire new skills such as empathy, compassion and generosity, and you will improve your reading skills.

PEACE
is the
WAY

5

CHAPTER 1

Jesus in the magical world

Once upon a time, in a far away place, there was a child named Jesus. Jesus was born in a humble stable in Bethlehem. From birth, Jesus was known to be special. The animals surrounded him calmly and serenely, and a bright star lit up the sky above the barn. Jesus grew up in Nazareth, surrounded by the love of his parents, Joseph and Mary, and his siblings and friends. From a very young age,

Jesus always showed extraordinary wisdom and kindness, and his presence radiated peace and love around him. Jesus liked to walk trought the magical world, where fairies, unicorns, and elves were his friends.

9

One day, while walking through the forest, Jesus heard a fairy crying. He approached her and asked what happened to her. The fairy replied that her magic wand was broken and she could not fix it.

10

Jesus took the wand and thought it over carefully. Then, using his wisdom, he fixed it in the blink of an eye. The fairy was very grateful and promised to grant her whatever wish she wanted. Jesus did not ask for anything for himself,

11

instead he asked that all magical beings in the kingdom have a safe and happy home. The fairy smiled and told her that her wishes had been granted. From that day on, all magical beings had a cozy and loving home.

One day, Jesus was in the village of the kingdom, when he heard a woman crying. He approached her and asked what happened to her. The woman replied that her son was very sick and she did not know what to do. Jesus asked if he could see the child.

13

When Jesus saw the child, he knew immediately what he had to do. His warm and comforting hands rested on the body of the sick child. With his magical wisdom and immense love, Jesus sent healing energy through his hands, filling the boy with bright, vibrant light.

14

The boy began to feel a sense of calm and strength within him. The illness that had debilitated him gradually began to fade, replaced by a renewed sense of vitality and health. Colors returned to her face and her eyes sparkled with joy.

15

The woman was very grateful and asked Jesus who he was. Jesus smiled and told him that he was a friend of the magical beings and that he had come to help. The woman promised to tell the whole kingdom about his goodness.

16

The woman was very grateful and asked Jesus who he was. Jesus smiled and told him that he was a friend of the magical beings and that he had come to help. The woman promised to tell the whole kingdom about his goodness.

16

The boy began to feel a sense of calm and strength within him. The illness that had debilitated him gradually began to fade, replaced by a renewed sense of vitality and health. Colors returned to her face and her eyes sparkled with joy.

15

The woman she left very grateful. Jesus became a hero in the magical kingdom and everyone loved him and followed him wherever he went. Jesus acquired his wisdom and his goodness to help everyone who needed his help.

11

Never asked for anything in return, I just wanted to make the world a better place. And so, Jesus experienced happily ever after in the magical kingdom, helping everyone who needed his help and sharing his love and wisdom with the world.

18

CHAPTER 2
Message of peace in the village

Jesus lived in a small town surrounded by mountains and green fields. His parents, José and María, were very humble and hard-working people who cared a lot about him.

From an early age, Jesus showed a great interest in learning and helping others, and his charisma and kindness were contagious.One day, while Jesus was walking through the field, he met an old man who looked very sad.

Jesus approached him and asked him what happened to him. The man replied that he had lost his house and all his belongings in a fire, and now he had nowhere to go.

22

Jesus asked if he could help in any way, and the man asked him to help him find a place where he could sleep that night.Jesus decided to take the man to his own home.

Despite the fact that his family was very humble and did not have much space, they did everything possible to make the man feel comfortable and safe. They fed him and gave him a bed to sleep on.

24

The man was very
grateful and asked
Jesus who he was.
Jesus just smiled and
said that he was a
friend who was there
to help. The next day,
Jesus went to work
in the fields with his
father.

While they were working, hearing a woman screaming for help. They ran to where the woman was and saw that her daughter had fallen into a well and couldn't get out.

Joseph and Jesus worked together to pull the girl out of the well, and she was safe and uninjured. The girl's mother was very grateful and asked Jesus who he was. Jesus just smiled and said that he was a friend who was there to help.

As Jesus grew older, his reputation for doing good and helping others grew throughout the town. People come to him for advice or help in times of need. He was always there to listen and offer a kind word or friendly gesture.

28

One day, a group of bandits invaded the town. They robbed people and caused destruction everywhere. Jesús and his father José cannot sit idly by, so they joined the other villagers to drive out the bandits.

29

They fought together to defend their home and protect their loved ones. When the bandits finally withdrew, the people were grateful for their bravery and courage. They had learned a powerful lesson:

30

when they come together and support each other, they can overcome any obstacle and face any challenge. In the midst of the celebration, Jesus approached the crowd with a radiant smile.

31

They all gathered around him, eager to express their appreciation and curiosity for his presence at this crucial moment. Jesus shared stories of love, compassion, and hope, inspiring everyone to be brave and kind.

32

CHAPTER 3

A great day on Easter Island

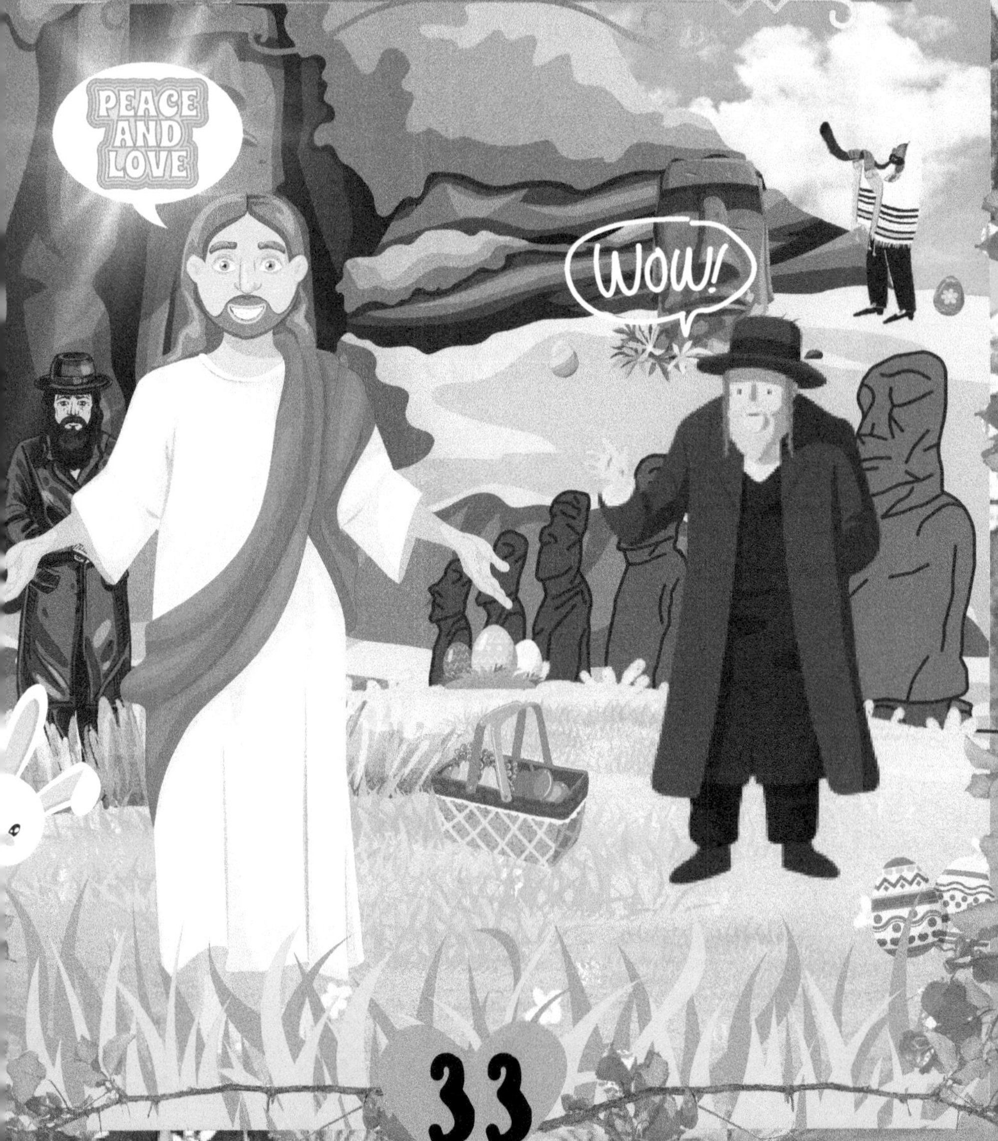

From a very young age, Jesus had shown a great interest in learning and helping others, and his charisma and kindness were contagious. Jesus had a large family: his parents, Joseph and Mary, and his brothers and sisters, who loved and cared for him.

34

One day, when Jesus was twelve years old, his parents took him to the temple to celebrate the Passover festival. There, Jesus met the rabbis, who had great knowledge of the Scriptures and spoke with great wisdom.

35

Jesus listened carefully to everything they said and asked questions that surprised everyone. The rabbis were amazed by Jesus' knowledge and understanding of the Scriptures. His wisdom shone like a star in the sky.

36

With humility, Jesus explained to them that their knowledge came from a deep connection with God and his love for all people. He taught them that the true power of Scripture was not just in its interpretation,

but in how those
words could
transform lives and
bring hope.
During those days,
Jesus understood that
his true mission in life
was to teach others
love and kindness. He
began to speak to the
people of his town,

38

sharing his wisdom
and teachings with
all who would
listen.
The fame of Jesus
will harden quickly
in the town and the
surrounding area.
People come from
far and wide to
hear him speak,

39

and soon his reputation will be deteriorating across the country. Jesus continued to teach, but he also helped others in any way he could. He healed the sick, fed the hungry, and helped those in need.

Although Jesus'
fame hardened
quickly and people
came from far and
wide to hear him
speak,
some began to
envy him and want
to stop him.
Despite this,

Jesus continued to teach and help those in need, healing the sick and feeding the hungry. His kindness and wisdom never diminished. Every day, Jesus was surrounded by people of all ages,

42

who came to hear his teachings and receive his loving support. Children in particular were drawn to him, fascinated by his charisma and his way of conveying profound messages with simple words.

CHAPTER 4

Jesus and true happiness

As Jesus grew, his fame spread throughout the country, and people came to him to hear his teachings and for advice. Jesus never got tired of helping others, and he always found the right words to give comfort and hope to those who needed it.

45

One day, a very rich man approached Jesus and asked him: "Master, what should I do to be happy? I have everything I could wish for, but I feel that something is missing."

46

Jesus replied, "True happiness is not found in riches, but in love and compassion for others. Help those who are in need, give comfort to the sad, and bring joy to those around you. If you do this you will find true happiness."

47

The rich man was
surprised by
Jesus' response,
but he decided to
follow his advice.
He began helping
the needy,
visiting the sick,
and bringing joy
to the sad.

48

Soon, I discovered that the happiness I had been looking for was in love and compassion for others. Jesus continued to teach and help others in any way he could. He healed the sick, fed the hungry and comforted the sad.

49

But not everyone was happy with his fame and his teachings. Some religious leaders began to envy him and wanted to stop him.One day, while Jesus was teaching in a public square, a group of men surrounded him and accused him of blasphemy. They wanted to arrest him and bring him before the authorities. But the crowd around him did not agree. Many had been healed by Jesus and had seen his goodness and love.

51

They decided to protect him and prevent him from being captured. A girl named Ana stepped forward and said in a firm voice, "Jesus has shown compassion and taught us to love one another.

He cannot be guilty of blasphemy. " His words resonated in everyone's hearts, reminding them of the importance of empathy and respect. The crowd, united in their support for Jesus, formed a human shield around him.

Their love and courage were so strong that the accusing men were forced back, unable to overcome the determination of the people. Jesus looked at the crowd with gratitude and spoke in a soft but firm voice:

"Thank you all for standing up for what is right and for remembering the values we have shared. Together, we can change the world with love and understanding." The crowd cheered, filling the air with applause and joy.

They knew that they had demonstrated the power of love and unity. From that day on, the community became even stronger, pledging to follow Jesus' example and spread his message of love and compassion throughout the world.

CHAPTER 5
Conference on the hill

57

From a very young age, Jesus showed exceptional wisdom and kindness that demonstrated him in a very loved person in his community.One day, Jesus met with his friends and followers on a hill near the town.

58

He knew that there was much to teach them, and he wanted to share with them God's teachings. So, together with his friends, he went up the hill and sat down in front of the crowd that had gathered there to listen to him.

Jesus began to talk about love and mercy, and taught them how to live their lives according to God's commandments. They spoke to them about the importance of loving their neighbor as oneself,

60

and asked them to always treat others with respect and compassion.
The people listened attentively to Jesus' words, and many of them felt deeply inspired to change their lives and follow him.

Jesus also spoke
to them about
the importance
of having faith in
God, and of
trusting in him at
all times, even in
the most
difficult
moments.

The days passed,
and Jesus
continued
teaching and
helping the people
of his town. He
healed the sick,
fed the hungry,
and comforted
the afflicted.

63

The fame of Jesus quickly spread throughout the country, and people flocked to him from everywhere to hear him speak and receive his help.

64

However, not everyone was happy with Jesus' teachings. There were those who saw him as a threat to their power and control over the people. They began to conspire against him.

CHAPTER 6
Jesus is arrested on the hill

One day, while Jesus was teaching his followers on a hill, a group of armed men came to arrest him. Jesus was arrested and brought before the governor of the country. Despite being falsely accused,

Jesus never lost his faith in God, and always maintained his love and compassion for others. The religious leaders had sent these men to arrest Jesus and they came before the Roman governor.

68

The followers of Jesus tried to resist, but Jesus told them not to fight, that this was God's will. He was brought before the Roman governor, who asked him many questions. Although Jesus knew his life was in danger, he never lost his cool or composure. The Roman governor found no fault with Jesus and could not understand why the religious leaders wanted to arrest him. But the crowd that had gathered in the street began to demand his execution.

10

The governor tried to free Jesus, but the crowd refused to accept his decision and demanded that he be crucified. Jesus knew that his mission was to do God's will, even if it meant dying.

11

He was sentenced to death by crucifixion and would be taken to a mountain called Golgotha, where he would finally be nailed to the cross.

CHAPTER 7

The crucifixion of jesus

13

Finally Jesus was taken to Golgotha, a hill outside the city, where he was crucified along with two robbers. Despite the pain and suffering, Jesus kept his faith and his love for humanity.

14

While Jesus was on the cross, many people were released around him, crying and lamenting his painful death. His friends and followers were heartbroken, not understanding why their master had to suffer so much.

15

But Jesus spoke to them with words of comfort and love, telling them that all of this was happening for a reason and that God was with them at this difficult time.

16

Some of those present, even those who had demanded his crucifixion, were deeply moved by Jesus' words and began to understand the message he had been trying to convey.

They began to see the love and kindness in his teachings and regretted having condemned him.As he lay dying on the cross, Jesus worried about his mother,

18

who was among
those with him.
He asked one of
his followers to
take care of her
as if she were his
own
mother.Despite
the pain and
suffering,

Jesus kept his faith and his love for humanity. In his last moments, he said: "Father, forgive them, for they do not know what they are doing." The earth shook and the skies darkened as Jesus died on the cross.

After his death, Jesus was buried in a tomb, People wept and mourned his death, but Jesus knew that his sacrifice would not be in vain.

RIP

81

CHAPTER 8
Jesus rises on the third day

The tomb was empty, and people started talking about how Jesus had risen from the dead. His friends and followers couldn't believe what they heard, but then they saw it with their own eyes.

Jesus appeared to
them, filling
them with joy
and hope.On the
third day after
his death, Jesus
rose from the
dead and
appeared to his
followers.

84

He told them that love
and kindness were
stronger than death,
and that he would
always be with them,
guiding and protecting
them.Jesus' followers
were surprised and
overjoyed to see him
alive again.

85

They hugged him with tears in their eyes and could not believe that their beloved leader had come back to life. Jesus spoke to them and told them that they were not afraid,

that he was there
with them
forever. They
were taught that
death is not the
end, that there is
life after death,
and that those who
believe in God will
live forever.

For forty days, Jesus appeared to his followers and taught them many things. They spoke to them about love, kindness, mercy, and justice, and asked them to share their teachings with the whole world.

88

He told them that he would spread his message of hope and peace, and help others whenever he could. After forty days, Jesus ascended to heaven, but he promised that he would return one day.

His followers were left with their hearts full of joy and hope, knowing that their beloved leader was with them always, guiding and protecting them from heaven.

90

CHAPTER 9
The great message of Jesus

91

The story of Jesus
became a legend
that has been
passed down from
generation to
generation. Jesus
became a symbol of
love, hope and
goodness for all
people,

and his message
continues to
resonate in the
hearts of those
who seek truth
and peace. The
story of Jesus
continued to
inspire many
people through
the years.

93

His teachings on love and kindness spread throughout the world, and many men and women leaned on his followers.Over time, churches and cathedrals were built in his honor,

94

and books and
songs were
written about his
life and message.
People gathered in
these churches to
worship him and
remember his
legacy.

In many countries, the day of his birth was celebrated as an important holiday, known as Christmas. The story of Jesus has also been a great comfort to those who have suffered loss and pain.

96

It has given them hope that death is not the end and that, like Jesus, they too can find life after death. But perhaps most important of all, the story of Jesus reminds us that love and kindness are stronger than anything else in the world.

It reminds us that despite pain and suffering, there is always a light at the end of the tunnel. And it teaches us that even in the darkest of times, we must keep the faith and keep going.

Today there are
many people who
follow in the
footsteps of Jesus
and try to live their
lives following his
teachings. They are
people who do good
to others, who try
to be fair and kind,

and who seek truth and wisdom in everything they do. The story of Jesus also reminds us that love and compassion are stronger than hate and violence. It teaches us that although it may sometimes seem like evil is in control, good will always ultimately prevail. So although the story of Jesus is ancient, it is still relevant today. It gives us hope and strength to face life's challenges and reminds us that love and kindness are always possible.

END

Dear friend,

I hope you enjoyed this story about the life of Jesus. It has been an honor to be able to share with you this story full of love, compassion and valuable teachings.

Let us always remember the example of Jesus and apply his teachings in our daily lives. By loving and respecting others, we can contribute to making the world a better place.

I sincerely appreciate the opportunity to have created this story for you. I am always here to answer your questions and to help you in any other literary adventure you wish to undertake.

May the light and love of Jesus always guide your steps.